A NOTE TO PARENTS

Early Step into Reading Books are designed for preschoolers and kindergartners who are just getting ready to read. The words are easy, the type is big, and the stories are packed with rhyme, rhythm, and repetition.

We suggest that you read this book to your child the first few times, pointing to each word as you go. Soon your child will start saying the words with you. And before long, he or she will try to read the story alone. Don't be surprised if your child uses the pictures to figure out the text—that's what they're there for! The important thing is to develop your child's confidence—and to show your child that reading is fun.

When your child is ready to move on, try the rest of the steps in our Step into Reading series. **Step 1 Books** (preschool–grade 1) feature the same easy-to-read type as the Early Step into Reading Books, but with more words per page. **Step 2 Books** (grades 1–3) are both longer and slightly more difficult, while **Step 3 Books** (grades 2–3) introduce readers to paragraphs and fully developed plot lines. **Step 4 Books** (grades 2–4) offer exciting nonfiction for the increasingly independent reader.

The grade levels assigned to the five steps are intended only as guides. Some children move through all five steps very rapidly; others climb the steps over a period of several years. Either way, these books will help your child "step into reading" in style!

For Snowy   *—A. R.*

Library of Congress Cataloging-in-Publication Data
Rockwell, Anne. Sweet potato pie / by Anne Rockwell ; illustrated by Carolyn Croll.
  p. cm. — (Early step into reading)
SUMMARY: Everybody on the farm stops what they are doing to come and enjoy Grandma's
sweet potato pie.
ISBN 0-679-86440-7 (pbk.) — ISBN 0-679-96440-1 (lib. bdg.)
[1. Baking—Fiction. 2. Farm life—Fiction. 3. Stories in rhyme.]
I. Croll, Carolyn, ill. II. Title. III. Series.
PZ8.3.R597Sw 1996 [E]—dc20 94-34990

Manufactured in the United States of America   10 9 8 7 6 5 4 3 2 1

STEP INTO READING is a trademark of Random House, Inc.

Early Step into Reading™

Sweet Potato Pie

by Anne Rockwell
illustrated by Carolyn Croll

Random House   New York

4

Pa picks sweet potatoes
one by one.

Why, oh, why?
Sweet potato pie!

Grandma bakes them

till they're done.

Why, oh, why?
Sweet potato pie!

Gramps stops chopping.

Ma stops washing.

Tom stops swimming.

Why, oh, why?

Sis stops swinging.

Bob starts singing.

COME AND GET MY
SWEET POTATO PIE!

Everybody coming
one by one.

Why, oh, why?
Sweet potato pie!

Everybody eating

till there's none.

My, oh, my.

Sweet potato pie!

E
ROC

Rockwell, Anne F.

Sweet potato pie.

Copy 2

$9.99